WORLD WAR II TALES
THE BIKE ESCAPE

This book is for the real Harry Burdess

First published 2015 by
A & C Black, an imprint of Bloomsbury Publishing Plc
50 Bedford Square
London WC1B 3DP

www.bloomsbury.com

Bloomsbury is a registered trademark of Bloomsbury Publishing Plc

Text copyright © 2015 Terry Deary
Illustrations copyright © 2015 James de la Rue

The rights of Terry Deary and James de la Rue to be identified as the
author and illustrator of this work have been asserted by them in
accordance with the Copyrights, Designs and Patents Act 1988.

ISBN 978-1-4729-1624-2

A CIP catalogue for this book is available from the British Library.

Printed and Bound by CPI Group (UK) Ltd, Croydon CR0 4YY

1 3 5 7 9 10 8 6 4 2

WORLD WAR II TALES

TERRY DEARY

THE BIKE ESCAPE

Illustrated by James de la Rue

A & C BLACK
AN IMPRINT OF BLOOMSBURY
LONDON NEW DELHI NEW YORK SYDNEY

Chapter 1
Chalk and cheese

October 1939, Highgate, London

It all started when I stole one piece of chalk. Mr Denton our teacher wasn't looking and I stole his chalk. Not all of it. Just a new stick of bright white chalk. My friend Myra Dodds kept watch at the door.

'He's out of sight, Harry!' she said in a whisper loud enough to wake half of Highgate Cemetery. You don't want to wake up the dead in Highgate Cemetery. They say one of Dracula's victims is buried there. It gives me the creeps.

Anyway, Myra watched Mr Denton go down the corridor and into the staff room. I opened the door to his cupboard, found the box of chalk and pulled it off the shelf. The blackboard rubber fell off the top of the box and hit me in the chest. It clattered onto the floor and left a white cloud to settle quietly. I didn't notice the white mark on my school tie.

There were three sticks of chalk left in the box. I slipped one into the pocket of my grey jacket. I picked up the rubber and put the box back where

I'd found it. Then I ran out of the classroom to join the lads in a game of football.

There weren't a lot of lads left in the school. As soon as the war started in September that year they shipped half of the kids into the countryside. Evacuees, they called them. Mr Denton, the head teacher, had stood up in assembly with his serious face on. 'When the war starts Mr Hitler will send his bombers to drop bombs on London.' He stopped. He looked around. He waited for us to start shaking with fear and screaming.

I think I just looked bored. 'My mum says he won't waste his bombs on Highgate,' I muttered to Myra.

Mr Denton glared at me. He went on, 'The children of London will be sent to the countryside where they will be safe.

When you go home this afternoon you will have a letter for your parents giving you the details. You will pack a small suitcase, take your gas mask, and bring them to school. Get your mums to make you some cheese sandwiches too. A bus will take you to your new home somewhere in England or Wales.'

I shook my head. 'My mum says we don't *have* to go if we don't want to. My mum says I'm staying. My mum says it's safe.'

'Your mum says a lot,' Myra said.

8

'Suppose so,' I agreed. What she said was true.

So most of the boys and girls went off looking more miserable than a wet dog, but I stayed. I could have stayed the whole war if it hadn't been for that bit of chalk.

I just wanted to chalk a goal on the wall of our back alley so we could play football.

I didn't think I'd get caught, did I?

Chapter 2
Time and crime

We kicked a shabby tennis ball around the school yard until the whistle went and we had to line up at the school entrance. We walked in silently to queue again outside the classroom door. Mr Denton marched down the corridor. His black teacher's gown swirled and smelled of cigarettes and chalk dust.

We stood at our desks until he told us to sit and then he stared at the floor and the mark left by the blackboard rubber. He turned quietly to his cupboard and took out the box of chalks. If there had been twenty sticks in the box he wouldn't have missed one. But there were two. There should have been three.

'Stand,' he barked. Chairs clattered as we stood. He walked slowly down the aisle looking at us with the eyes of a hawk. He stopped when he reached me, glanced at the chalk mark on my tie and thrust a hand into my jacket pocket. He pulled out the chalk and waved it under my nose. 'Mine, I think?'

'It hasn't got your name on it, sir,' I said.

His hand was so fast I didn't see it move but I felt the pain as it smacked my left ear. He breathed through his tobacco-stained teeth. 'The boy who steals chalk today steals from shops tomorrow. He grows up to steal from houses and then he robs banks. And where does he end up?'

'Rich?' I said.

I was ready for the slap on my left ear but this time he caught me out by hitting the other side of my head. I almost fell over. I wondered if they taught teachers the tricks of how to slap heads and cane hands when they went to college.

'The thief ends up in prison. Just like your father,' he hissed. 'And it all starts with stealing chalk from school. So I am going to do you a favour, young Burdess. I am going to teach you a lesson. When you have learned that it is wrong to steal, you may be saved from a life of crime.'

I thought he was going to cane me. That would be my 'lesson'. I was wrong. Again.

'After school I will come to your house with Constable Wright. We will have a word with your poor mother.' His hand reached up and grabbed the short hair in front of my ear and tugged at it till my eyes watered. 'Then we'll see what happens to thieves.'

13

He strutted to the front of the class with a smirk on his face.

As I walked home that night I tried to act as if I didn't care. 'I won't go to prison. Not for stealing a piece of chalk,' I said to Myra Dodds as we reached the street corner and leaned against the bin they put there to collect pig food.

'They'll just tell you off,' Myra said. 'You won't be sent to prison.'

'Suppose so,' I agreed. I didn't know I was going to be sent somewhere much worse.

Chapter 3
Biscuits and bombs

My mum was cross. 'I'll have to tidy the front parlour if we have the copper coming round. What on earth were you thinking of, pinching chalk? Eh?' she said as she rubbed a duster over the table.

'Sorry, Mum.'

'If you're going to start pinching stuff why can't you pinch something useful, like food – a pound of sausages for our tea – or a new dress for me? Your dad would be ashamed of you. Chalk!' she squawked and spat in one of our best china cups to rub off a mark with her duster.

'Mr Denton can have that cup,' I said.

'The tea leaves are in the pot, pour on the boiling water. I haven't got any cakes or scones to give them,' she moaned. 'I don't have enough ration coupons. They can have some of those old ginger biscuits I bought before the war.'

'Mum, they're coming here to shout at me, not to have a teddy-bear's picnic.'

'I'll not have them saying I have a dirty house,' she said and spat into another cup. She took off her headscarf and took out her hair rollers – she only did that when she went to visit Dad. I made the tea.

PC Wright was almost too tall and wide to fit in our doorway but he kept his helmet on as he sat at the table. Mr Denton was like a grey eel beside him as he slimed his way into the best room.

Mum poured the tea as the policeman spoke in a deep brown voice, like a judge that was going to send a man to be hanged. Mum pushed the plate of stale biscuits across the table and wrapped her pinafore tight around her. 'So? Are you sending our Harry to prison or not?' she asked.

PC Wright looked at the teacher who gave an oily smile. 'I was thinking of how we could spare the lad,' he said.

'What?' Mum asked, almost as surprised as I was.

'Many young evacuees have left the school to go to the country where it is safe from bombs,' Mr Denton went on.

'I haven't seen any bombs,' Mum argued. 'We have shelters in the back yards and on the waste ground. We have those sirens going off at all hours. We have searchlights and barrage balloons. We have everything except bombs.'

'They will come,' PC Wright rumbled.

'The point is,' Mr Denton said, 'you have a choice. You can send the boy away as an evacuee, or we can charge him with theft.' The teacher looked as happy as a dog with a leg of lamb. He wanted rid of me from his school and this was his chance. I was sure Mum would stand up to him and tell him to go to...well.

Mum scowled. 'You can send Harry off as an evacuee,' she said sourly.

'No, Mum!' I wailed.

'You can leave tomorrow,' Mr Denton said.

Chapter 4
Wizard and War

I had seen the pictures in the newspapers. The children who were evacuated. Little angels in their best clothes, holding hands. Labels and gas masks around their necks. Little suitcases with a change of clothes and a jam sandwich. Tears. Waves. Sobbing mothers and steaming trains pulling away from cold platforms.

I heard about what happened at the other end. The kids in our street sent letters home from their new homes. They said the hosts picked the cleanest, prettiest

little girls first and the scruffy lads were left till last. They said it was like a slave market. They said the country kids in the villages hated them and called them 'vaccies', not evacuees.

Myra Dodds said her brother was evacuated and thought he stepped off the train into a war. The local children said the London kids talked funny and called them 'Townies' or 'slum kids'. The evacuees called the locals 'yokels' or 'clodhoppers' or 'turnips'. There were battles with throwing mud and stones and sticks. In the end they sent the evacuees to school in the mornings and the locals in the afternoon so they wouldn't fight. Of course the locals just lay in ambush, waiting for the vaccies to walk home at dinner time.

But I wasn't in the swarms of screaming kids. I was sent off by myself. Mum took me to the station half an hour early. 'I'll not wait to wave you off. It's cold on this platform.'

'Yeah, you go home, Mum,' I said.

'You got your book that Mr Benton gave you to read on the train? He said it would do you good to read it.'

'Yes, Mum,' I sighed. The book was called *Great Expectations* and it started off all right but it was hard work. I had

a copy of *Wizard* comic in my gas-mask box. That would be better. It had a picture on the cover of a giant beetle attacking a man and exciting war stories inside. And I borrowed a copy of *The Skipper* comic from the newspaper shop – I knew Captain Zoom: Birdman of the RAF would win the war for us.

Mr Denton had also given me a map book to study. 'Geography,' he said.

'And have you got that clean handkerchief? It was one of your dad's. Look after it.'

'Yes, Mum.'

With a wave she was gone. The station clock ticked round. Fifteen minutes to go. A troop of soldiers crowded into my carriage with kit-bags and rifles. The cigarette smoke was choking. I stepped into the corridor and pulled down a window.

I saw a girl push past the ticket collector and run down the platform. She had two untidy bunches in her hair, each tied with a different ribbon. She saw me and grinned. 'Hello, Myra,' I said. 'Are you being evacuated?'

'No,' she panted. 'I just came to say

24

goodbye. I missed you in class and Mr Denton said you were being sent away. I had to say goodbye.'

She looked pink and awkward. I didn't know what to say. So I said, 'Goodbye.'

'Can we write letters while you're away?'

'I suppose,' I muttered. 'If they let me have stamps and paper.'

'You could tear a sheet from your school exercise book,' she said.

'Suppose,' I said.

'See you soon,' she said. A daft thing to say.

Then a whistle blew and the train sent out clouds of steam and smoke as it pulled away. Myra was hidden in its fog. When it cleared a minute later she was waving. The smoke seemed to be making my eyes water. I waved back. 'See you soon,' I shouted.

Chapter 5

Polish and pyjamas

The train took six hours to travel just sixty miles. There was no slave market at the end of it, no evacuees on the draughty platform except me. A pale and pinch-faced woman in a green coat and a purple hat was waiting for me. She was old enough to be my granny. She might have been a hundred. I was just glad to get off the train.

'I'm Miss Pimm,' she said. 'The vicar of our church asked me to take you in, Harry.'

She gave a smile that was vinegar thin. I could tell she was trying to be friendly. She just didn't know how. 'Do I have to go to church?' I asked.

She turned paler. 'We all have to go to church, Harry. Let's go and get you some tea, shall we?'

'Suppose,' I said.

Her house was a terraced one like ours but it smelled of furniture polish and lavender. Everything was so clean it made me feel dirty. Mum's house was a bit of a mess to be honest. My bed in Miss Pimm's spare room had clean white sheets. Miss Pimm said I should have a bath before I went to bed. I knew why.

As I went into the bathroom she handed me some shampoo for my nits. 'The London evacuees often come with nits,' she twittered like a bird. 'Nothing wrong with nits, but the local children often pick on the London children because of them. Better safe than sorry.'

She wanted to be kind, I suppose. At least the bath was a proper one – not the tin tub we had to use in front of the fire back home. I soaked for a long time before I stepped out and went downstairs in the

pyjamas and dressing gown the church had found for me.

Miss Pimm listened to the radio while I opened Mr Denton's map book and began to study it.

She cleared her throat with a chirp like a sparrow. 'The vicar said you...erm...had been in a little trouble back in Highbury. Some stealing, I believe. I am a poor old lady. There's nothing in the house worth stealing. If you want anything, ask and maybe the vicar will find it for you?'

I just looked at her. So Mr Denton had warned them about me, had he? 'What's this place called?' I asked.

'Wootton, near Northampton,' she said.

I found it on the map. I used my clean finger to trace a line down a road marked in green on the map. The road was called the A45. At a place called Towcester it joined the A5 and that led straight back to London.

I smiled at her. 'What's this road called? The one you live on?'

'London Road,' she said.

Perfect. Couldn't be better. I slept well that night in the soft, clean sheets and dreamed of escapes as daring as Captain Zoom's...except I didn't have his wings.

Chapter 6
Straps and saddles

The local turnip kids were no problem. They called me names but as soon as I turned and stared at them they ran away. It was the London kids in the Wootton village school who were worse. They'd been there in Wootton a month and formed their own little gangs and groups of friends. I was the outsider. And I was from North London, they were from the East End of London – another world.

I could list the miseries but it would bore you, and I want to forget them. The teacher was worse than Mr Denton. She was called Miss Sparling and she used a strap instead of a cane. Then there was the vicar, Reverend O'Brien, who raged at me for my thieving past, and the policeman, Constable Grey, who watched me like a snake watches a rabbit.

The one thing I looked forward to was the end of the day. At the corner of Miss Pimm's road a gang of young women gathered at the end of each day. Buses dropped them off and they met up to smoke and gossip.

They all wore trousers – I'd never seen a woman in trousers. One day, when I'd been in Wootton a week, I guess I gawped at them too long. 'What's the matter, lad, never seen a beautiful woman before?' one of them asked me. She had wavy red hair and she wasn't all that pretty. But she was cheerful and friendly, not like the rest of Wootton.

'Are you in the army?'

'The Land Army,' she said. 'We help out on the farms while the men are away fighting. I'm Ellen.'

'I'm Harry,' I said and we shook hands.

'Is that your bike?' I asked. It was painted black and the wheels were crusted with mud, but it looked like Dad's getaway car to me.

'Yes. I need it to get around the farm – I have to set a dozen rat traps every day. I have to cycle miles.'

'Can I have a go?'

'Catching rats?'

'No. Riding your bike,' I said.

She reached into the little leather bag at the back of the saddle and took out a spanner. She lowered the saddle so it was right for me. I set off down the road and pedalled hard to see how fast I could go. Then I turned back and pulled up beside red-haired Ellen. 'Can I borrow it?' I asked.

She shrugged. 'It's not mine. It's the farmer's. What do you need it for?'

I sighed. There was no point telling her. But she had a kind face. I thought she might understand. So I told her my problem.

Chapter 7

Fence and firewood

I told Ellen what had happened the day before.

Old Miss Pimm had been kind to me in her own odd way. I wanted to be kind to her.

Leaves were tumbling off the trees and the wind from the East was icy. Miss Pimm had a miserable little fire of coal dust. I sat there with the *Wizard* comic and heard her false teeth chattering.

Those winds had snapped a tree branch and it lay on waste ground just down the road. On the weekend I climbed through a gap in the fence with a saw I found in her back-yard shed. She said the saw belonged to her dead brother. I sawed the branch into logs and took them back for her fire. It was good to see her warm and comfy, listening to Winston Churchill speaking on the radio.

The next day there was a hammering on the door as I was just about to leave for school. Constable Grey stood there with a cruel leer on his ugly face. 'Hello, Miss Pimm,' he said. 'I have reason to believe your little vaccie is a thief.'

The old lady gasped. 'What's he done now?'

'Stolen a branch from private land. Cut it up for firewood.'

'No!' she moaned. 'Oh, Harry, you told me the logs were from waste ground.'

'They are.'

Constable Grey puffed out his chest and spoke like a vicar. 'The land in question is enclosed by a fence. It is enclosed by a fence to show it is private land. The tree is private property.'

'The fence was broken,' I argued.

The policeman leaned forward and snarled, 'Your front door could be broken but that does not mean anyone can walk in and help themselves to your property.'

'It was a miserable little branch,' I cried. 'A branch that the owner of the tree could have cut up and burned. Now you are coming back to school with me and Miss Sparling will deal with you.'

The strap didn't hurt that much. But the laughter of my 'friends' from London did. And they refused to let me join their football at break time. 'Watch out. Burdess might steal the ball,' they sniggered.

'Fasten your belt tight or Burdess might steal your trousers.' *Giggle.*

When no teacher was around they took it in turns to kick me and run away. It was a miserable day.

I told all this to the Land Girl, Ellen. 'So what will you do if I lend you the bike? You can't run away from the bullies.'

'I can,' I said. 'I know a place to go.'

'It's not my bike,' she said. 'I can't lend it. But if you ride off on it I can't stop you, can I?' She gave me a wink. I grinned. I stood up in the pedals and pushed off down the road. I had Mr Denton's map book tucked into my belt. I was heading south down London Road.

Constable Grey stepped off the pavement when I reached the crossroads and held up a hand for me to stop. I went faster. 'Where are you going?' he roared.

'None of your business, fat-face,' I laughed, and the wind carried me and my words along the road to freedom.

Chapter 8
Lights and lorry

It soon grew dark but the road was wide and the starlight bright enough to guide me. I began to feel the cold. My short trousers and school jacket didn't keep out the cold and I pulled down the sleeves of my jumper to wrap around my hands like gloves. It meant I couldn't grip the brakes quickly but I didn't care.

I knew Mum would have the cooking range nice and hot. If I kept going I'd be home for breakfast.

There were only a few cars on the road

because the petrol was on ration. The headlamps showed a little light through slits in the masks over their headlights.

A few street lights spilled a glow from their masks. I stopped for breath underneath one to look at my map. I was in the small town of Towcester. I reckoned I'd done around ten miles in my first hour and was about to turn onto the A5.

As I slipped the map book back into

my belt a voice said, 'And where are you off to, young man?'

An ancient policeman was smiling down at me. Too old for the army, I thought, but good enough to hobble round the town and keep an eye out for trouble. 'Stony Stratford,' I said because that was the next place on my map. That was a mistake.

'You have no lights,' he reminded me.

'There's a blackout,' I said quickly. 'And I can see where I'm going.'

'That's not the point. Can a driver see *you*? There are army lorries that use the A5. They'll flatten you and not feel the bump. You'll be like strawberry jam on the road.'

'I'll be fine,' I said and shuffled from one cold foot to another.

At that moment I heard the rattle of a bell and a blue light flashed on a police box behind the old constable. 'Hang on a minute, son,' he said and crossed to the box. He opened the door and picked up a telephone. I put my foot softly on the pedal as I heard him speaking. Luckily he was a bit deaf and spoke too loud. 'Boy on a bike...headed for London...why, as it happens, yes...dangerous...thief... yes... Grey jacket and trousers? It's a bit dark to see but that sounds like him...black bike... yes...hold him till the Northampton police arrive?'

He put the phone down and crossed towards me. 'Now then, Harry, come along to the police station and I'll make you a nice hot cup of tea,' he said in a voice like a creaking parrot.

I pushed the pedal and glided away from the kerb as smooth as Captain Zoom. I made a large circle in the road.

'Come back here, lad,' he croaked. That was a daft thing to say. He hobbled across to me as I built up speed. 'Come here and I'll arrest you for having no lights on that cycle.' That was an even dafter thing to say.

I straightened the wheel and set off at speed down the main road to London. The excitement had me pedalling with legs like a windmill in a gale. But as I left the houses behind and headed into the blackness I began to tire.

The next hour was weary. My eyeballs were frozen and my legs getting weak. The heavy bike was wandering towards the white line in the middle of the road

and I was riding while half asleep. What woke me was the roar of a lorry coming around the bend in the road behind me.

I looked over my shoulder to see the narrow slits of light racing towards me. Enough light for me to see the lorry but not enough for the driver to see me.

I swerved to the left and my bike bounced on the grass verge. Before I could stop it I was sliding into a muddy ditch and the rattling lorry was thundering past.

And that's what saved me from being caught.

Chapter 9
Maps and mud

I heard the lorry brakes screech and the tyres scream on the road as it shuddered to a halt. There was a bellow of angry voices. The soldiers in the back had been thrown off their seats and the policemen in the middle of the road were telling the driver he'd been going too fast.

In the midst of the shouting I heard the words, 'Boy on a bike' and 'Road block'.

I crawled out of the ditch and wheeled the bike towards the crossroads. A police car was blocking the way. It was a trap and I was the one who was supposed to ride into it.

As the soldiers and the police raged at one another I found a gate into the field beside the road and headed south across the muddy, ploughed earth. Sometimes the mud was up to my ankles and sometimes the wheels of the heavy bike were stuck. But the coppers at the crossroads couldn't see me because of the hedge. It took me half an hour to walk a few hundred yards past the road block.

When I was sure the police lookouts were well behind me I joined the A5 again and pedalled south. I checked with the map to look for crossroads ahead – I thought that was where they'd try to catch me. I guessed right. There were police waiting at Bletchley and Dunstable but I was able to ride through the side streets to get around them.

The sun was rising as I reached a road sign that said 'London 5 miles' and I knew where I was. My weary legs found new strength and I raced for home. The shops were starting to open and there were cars and buses shuffling along.

PC Wright would be at the crossroads on traffic duty. I'd ride past him and thumb my nose. I was nearly home and Mum would be so pleased to see me she'd smother me in hugs and fill me full of hot, sweet tea.

But PC Wright wasn't on traffic duty. A big surprise. Never mind, I climbed stiffly

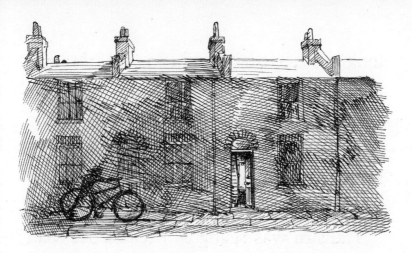

out of the saddle and wheeled my bike the last few yards down the road. Our front door was open. A bigger surprise.

From the parlour I heard Mum talking and a man's deep voice replied. Was Dad out of prison?

I threw the parlour door open and three pale faces looked at me. Serious faces. Cross faces. Faces I knew.

Mum was standing by the table with a pot of tea and in the two armchairs sat my dear teacher, Mr Denton, and my favourite policeman, PC Wright.

Mum was the first to speak – well, shout. 'What have you done this time, our Harry?'

'I've come home to see you, Mum.'

'You've only gone and stolen a bike,' she ranted. 'Stealing chalk is one thing but a bike will get you locked away for sure.'

'I only borrowed it,' I sighed.

'Then you can only take it back,' she snapped.

'Take it back? I can't ride sixty miles. I can hardly walk sixty yards,' I argued.

'You will return on the ten o'clock train tomorrow morning,' Mr Denton said with a sneering smile. 'You will take the bike with you and return it to the Land Girl you stole it from.'

PC Wright added, 'And if you ever try to run away again you will be charged with the theft.'

'The boy who steals chalk today steals bicycles tomorrow. He grows up to steal from houses and then he robs banks. And where does he end up?' Mr Denton crowed.

'Mum?' I wailed.

'Nothing I can do about it, Harry. Now get out of those muddy clothes. You're trampling dirt into my nice clean carpet,' she said.

'What clean carpet?' I asked. And that got me a slap around the ear.

Chapter 10
Mates and Myra

I cleaned myself up and at lunchtime went out to meet some of the friends I'd left in Highbury School. They all had stories to tell about our mates who'd been evacuees. Some had gone to great homes but others had far worse than mine with Miss Pimm. 'Go back, Harry,' one lad said. 'Old Dentures Denton will make it Hell for you if you stay.'

He was right of course. Even Myra Dodds was nodding. Last week she was sorry to see me go. Now she was telling me to go. Funny things, girls.

I slept badly that night. I was aching and stiff all over and my old bed seemed lumpy and foul after Miss Pimm's soft mattress.

My suitcase was still up in Wootton so I just had a few dripping sandwiches and a bottle of cold tea in a paper carrier-bag as I wheeled the bike down to the station next morning. Mum didn't bother to come with me this time. She just stood at the door to our house and waved. 'And you won't come back till the war's over, will you?'

'Suppose.' Thanks, Mum.

The station platform was quiet today with just a handful of soldiers and workmen. I was hoping to get a seat in a carriage this time.

I handed the bike to the guard to put in the van. He grumbled about the mud on the wheels as if his van was fit to invite King George in to tea.

'Carriage three, compartment seven,' he said.

'What? Can't I just sit where I want?' I asked.

'Don't argue. Just go to carriage three, compartment seven.'

I trudged along, counting the carriages. I felt as low as a worm's belly. Not even

Myra was there to wave me goodbye. Nobody cared about Harry Burdess.

I wiped my nose on my sleeve and felt my eyes start to water like they had last time I was on this platform. Must have been the smoke from the engine.

I reached carriage three and counted along to compartment seven. It was almost empty. In the far corner there was a girl with her hair in two bunches. She carried a gas mask in a box around her neck and her suitcase was up on the luggage rack.

She turned to face me as I slid the door open. 'Hello, Harry,' she said with a shy smile.

'Hello, Myra. You being evacuated?'

She nodded. 'It was boring staying home,' she said. 'And you never wrote a letter like you promised.'

'I never had a chance. I was only away a week.'

'Well this time I'm coming with you to Wootton. They said there's a nice lady called Miss Pimm will put me up. So, you see, you don't have to write me letters.'

'That's good,' I said.

'Are you pleased?' she asked.

I shrugged. 'Suppose,' I said.

Epilogue

The Bike Escape is based on a true story. Harry lived in Highbury, North London, and was evacuated to a village near Northampton. Local boys bullied him and even his efforts to help his hosts were punished – he sawed up some fallen branches for firewood but was accused of stealing the wood. He was punished at school for the offence and that was the last straw. He borrowed a Land Girl's bike and cycled the 65 miles home to London. It did him no good. His mother sent him straight back!

The bombs didn't arrive for another year and many evacuees returned home long before the end of the war. Their parents missed them and brought them home. Some like Harry ran away.

Thousands returned home after the war

and never managed to find their parents again. They were among the saddest victims of World War II.